Mr Salary

Faber Stories

Sally Rooney was born in 1991 and lives in Dublin. Her work has appeared in *The New Yorker*, *Granta*, *The White Review*, *The Dublin Review*, *The Stinging Fly*, Kevin Barry's *Stonecutter* and *The Winter Page* anthology. Her first novel, *Conversations with Friends*, was the most popular debut in the 2017 end-of-year round-ups. Her second novel, *Normal People*, was released to wide critical acclaim in 2018. Rooney was shortlisted for the *Sunday Times* EFG Short Story Award for 'Mr Salary' and was the winner of the *Sunday Times*/PFD Young Writer of the Year Award.

Sally Rooney

Mr Salary

Faber Stories

ff

First published in this single edition in 2019
by Faber & Faber Limited
Bloomsbury House
74–77 Great Russell Street
London WC1B 3DA
First published by Granta in *Granta 135: New Irish Writing* in 2016

Typeset by Faber & Faber Limited
Printed and bound by CPI Group (UK) Ltd, Croydon, CR0 4YY

A CIP record for this book
is available from the British Library

ISBN 978–0–571–35195–4

10 9 8 7 6 5 4 3 2

Nathan was waiting with his hands in his pockets beside the silver Christmas tree in the arrivals lounge at Dublin airport. The new terminal was bright and polished, with a lot of escalators. I had just brushed my teeth in the airport bathroom. My suitcase was ugly and I was trying to carry it with a degree of irony. When Nathan saw me he asked: What is that, a joke suitcase?

You look good, I said.

He lifted the case out of my hand. I hope people don't think this belongs to me now that I'm carrying it, he said. He was still wearing his work clothes, a very clean navy suit. Nobody would think the suitcase belonged to him, it was obvious. I was the one wearing black leggings with a hole in one knee, and I hadn't washed my hair since I left Boston.

You look unbelievably good, I said. You look better than last time I saw you even.

I thought I was in decline by now. Age-wise. You look OK, but you're young, so.

What are you doing, yoga or something?

I've been running, he said. The car's just out here.

Outside it was below zero and a thin rim of frost had formed on the corners of Nathan's windshield. The interior of his car smelled like air freshener and the brand of aftershave he liked to wear to 'events'. I didn't know what the aftershave was called but I knew what the bottle looked like. I saw it in drug-stores sometimes and if I was having a bad day I let myself screw the cap off.

My hair feels physically unclean, I said. Not just unwashed but actively dirty.

Nathan closed the door and put the keys in

the ignition. The dash lit up in soft Scandinavian colours.

You don't have any news you've been waiting to tell me in person, do you? he said.

Do people do that?

You don't have like a secret tattoo or anything?

I would have attached it as a JPEG, I said. Believe me.

He was reversing out of the parking space and onto the neat lit avenue leading to the exit. I pulled my feet up onto the passenger seat so that I could hug my knees against my chest uncomfortably.

Why? I said. Do you have news?

Yeah yeah, I have a girlfriend now.

I turned my head to face him extremely slowly, one degree after another, like I was a character in slow motion in a horror film.

What? I said.

Actually we're getting married. And she's pregnant.

Then I turned my face back to stare at the windshield. The red brake lights of the car in front surfaced through the ice like a memory.

OK, funny, I said. Your jokes are always very humorous.

I could have a girlfriend. Hypothetically.

But then what would we joke about together?

He glanced at me as the barrier went up for the car in front of us.

Is that the coat I bought you? he said.

Yes. I wear it to remind me that you're real.

Nathan rolled his window down and inserted a ticket into the machine. Through Nathan's window the night air was delicious and frosty. He looked over at me again after he rolled it up.

I'm so happy to see you I'm having trouble talking in my normal accent, he said.

That's OK. I was having a lot of fantasies about you on the plane.

I look forward to hearing them. Do you want to pick up some food on the way home?

I hadn't been planning to come back to Dublin for Christmas, but my father Frank was being treated for leukaemia at the time. My mother had died from complications after my birth and Frank had never remarried, so legally speaking he was my only real family. As I explained in my 'happy holidays' email to my new classmates in Boston, he was going to die now too.

Frank had problems with prescription drugs. During childhood I had frequently been left in the care of his friends, who gave me either no affection or else so much that I recoiled and scrunched up like a porcupine. We lived in the Midlands, and when I moved to Dublin for university Frank liked to call me up and talk to me about my late mother, whom he informed me was 'no saint'. Then he would ask if he could borrow some money. In my second year of college we ran out of savings and I could no longer pay rent, so my mother's family cast around for someone I could live with until my exams were over.

Nathan's older sister was married to an uncle of mine, that's how I ended up moving in with him. I was nineteen then. He was thirty-four and had a beautiful two-bedroom apartment where he lived alone with a granite-topped kitchen island. At the time he worked for a start-up that developed 'behavioural software', which had something to do with feelings and consumer responsiveness. Nathan told me he only had to make people feel things: making them buy things came later on in the process. At some point the company had been bought out by Google, and now they all made hilarious salaries and worked in a building with expensive hand dryers in the bathroom.

Nathan was very relaxed about me moving in with him; he didn't make it weird. He was clean, but not prudish, and a good cook. We developed interests in each other's lives. I took sides when factional disputes arose in his office and he bought me things I admired in shop windows. I was only supposed to stay until I finished my exams that summer, but I ended up living there for nearly three years. My college friends worshipped Nathan and couldn't understand why he spent so much money on me. I think I did understand, but I couldn't explain it. His own friends seemed to assume there was some kind of sordid arrangement involved, because when he left the room they made certain remarks toward me.

They think you're paying me for something, I told him.

That made Nathan laugh. I'm not really getting my money's worth, am I? he said. You don't even do your own fucking laundry.

At the weekend we watched *Twin Peaks* and smoked weed together in his living room, and when it got late he ordered in more food than either of us could possibly eat. One night he told me he could remember my christening.

He said they served a cake with a little baby made out of icing on the top.

A cute baby, he told me.

Cuter than me? I said.

Yeah well, you weren't that cute.

It was Nathan who paid for my flights home from Boston that Christmas. All I had to do was ask.

The next morning after my shower I stood letting my hair drip onto the bath mat, checking visiting hours on my phone. Frank had been moved to the hospital in Dublin for inpatient treatment after contracting a secondary infection during chemotherapy. He had to get antibiotics on a drip. Gradually, as the steam heat in the bathroom dissipated, a fine veil of goosebumps rose up over my skin, and in the mirror my reflection clarified and thinned until I could see my own pores. On weekdays, visiting hours ran from 6 to 8 p.m.

Since Frank was diagnosed eight weeks previously, I had spent my free time amassing an encyclopaedic knowledge of chronic lymphocytic leukaemia. There was practically nothing left about it that I didn't know. I graduated way past the booklets they printed for sufferers and onto the hard medical texts, online discussion groups for oncologists, PDFs of recent peer-reviewed studies. I wasn't under the illusion that this made me a good daughter, or even that I was doing it out of concern for Frank. It was in my nature to absorb large volumes of information during times of distress, like I could master the distress through intellectual dominance. This is how I learned how unlikely it was that

Frank would survive. He never would have told me himself.

Nathan took me Christmas shopping in the afternoon before the hospital visit. I buttoned up my coat and wore a large fur hat so as to appear mysterious through shop windows. My most recent boyfriend, whom I'd met at grad school in Boston, had called me 'frigid', but added that he 'didn't mean it in a sexual way'. Sexually I'm very warm and generous, I told my friends. It's just the other stuff where the frigidity comes through.

They laughed, but at what? It was my joke, so I couldn't ask them.

Nathan's physical closeness had a sedative effect on me, and as we moved from shop to shop, time skimmed past us like an ice skater. I had never had occasion to visit a cancer patient before. Nathan's mother had been treated for breast cancer sometime in the 1990s, but I was too young to remember that. She was healthy now and played a lot of golf. Whenever I saw her, she told me I was the apple of her son's eye, in those exact words. She had fastened on to this phrase, probably because it so lacked any sinister connotation. It would have been equally applicable to me if I had been Nathan's girlfriend or his daughter. I thought I could place myself pretty firmly on the girlfriend-to-daughter spectrum, but I had once overheard Nathan referring to me as his niece, a degree of removal I resented.

We went for lunch on Suffolk Street and put all our luxurious paper gift bags under the table. He let me order sparkling wine and the most expensive main course they had.

Would you grieve if I died? I asked him.

I can't hear a word you're saying. Chew your food.

I swallowed submissively. He watched me at first but then looked away.

Would it be a major bereavement for you if I died? I said.

The most major one I can think of, yeah.

Nobody else would grieve.

Lots of people would, he said. Don't you have classmates?

He was giving me his attention now so I took another bite of steak and swallowed it before continuing.

That's shock you're talking about, I said. I mean bereavement.

What about your ex-boyfriend that I hate?

Dennis? He would actually like it if I died.

OK, that's another discussion, said Nathan. I'm talking full-scale grief. Most 24-year-olds would leave behind a lot of mourners, that's all I'm saying. With me it's just you.

He seemed to consider this while I worked on the steak.

I don't like these conversations where you ask me to imagine your death.

Why not?

How would you like it if I died?

I just want to know you love me, I said.

He moved some salad around his plate with his cutlery. He used cutlery like a real adult, not shooting glances at me to check if I was admiring his technique. I always shot glances at him.

Remember New Year's Eve two years ago? I said.

No.

It's OK. The Yuletide is a very romantic time.

He laughed at that. I was good at making him laugh when he didn't want to. Eat your food, Sukie, he said.

Can you drop me to the hospital at six? I asked.

Nathan looked at me then as I knew he would. We were predictable to each other, like two halves of the same brain. Outside the restaurant window it had started to sleet, and under the orange street lights the wet flakes looked like punctuation marks.

Sure, he said. Do you want me to come in with you?

No. He'll resent your presence anyway.

I didn't mean for his benefit. But that's all right.

For the last several years, in the grip of a severe addiction to prescription opiates, Frank's mental state had wandered in and out of what you might call coherence. Sometimes on the phone he was his old self: complaining about parking tickets, or calling Nathan sarcastic names like 'Mr Salary'. They hated each other and I mediated their mutual hatred in a way that made me feel successfully feminine. Other times, Frank was replaced by a different man, a blank and somehow innocent person who repeated things meaninglessly and left protracted silences which I had to try and fill. I preferred the first one, who at least had a sense of humour.

Before he was diagnosed with leukaemia, I had been toying with describing Frank as an 'abusive father' when the subject came up at campus parties. I felt some guilt about that now. He was unpredictable, but I didn't cower in terror of him, and his attempts at manipulation, though heavy, were never effective. I wasn't vulnerable to them. Emotionally, I saw myself as a smooth, hard little ball. He couldn't get purchase on me. I just rolled away.

During a phone call, Nathan had once suggested that the rolling was a coping strategy on my part. It was eleven at night in Boston when I called, meaning it was four in the morning in Dublin, but Nathan always picked up.

Do I roll away from you? I said.

No, he said. I don't think I exert the requisite pressure.

Oh, I don't know. Hey, are you in bed?

Right now? Sure. Where are you?

I was in bed too. Not for the first time during these phone calls, I slipped my hand between my legs and Nathan pretended not to notice. I like the sound of your voice, I told him. After several entirely silent seconds, he replied: Yes, I know you do.

For the whole time we lived together he had never had a girlfriend, but occasionally he came home late and I could hear him through my bedroom wall having sex with other women. If I happened to meet the woman the following morning, I would discreetly inspect her for any physical resemblance to myself. This way I found that everyone in some sense looks like everyone else. I wasn't jealous. In fact I looked forward to these incidents on his behalf, though it was never clear to me if he enjoyed them that much.

For the last few weeks now Nathan and I had been sending each other emails about my flight details, what our plans for Christmas were, whether I had been in touch with Frank. I sent messages detailing my research, quoting from academic papers or cancer foundation websites. *In chronic leukaemia, the cells can mature partly but not completely,* the website said. *These cells may look fairly normal, but they are not.*

When we arrived outside the hospital that night and Nathan went to park, I said: You go. I'll walk home. He looked at me, with his hands on the steering wheel in exactly the correct position, as if I was his driving examiner.

Go, I said. The walk will be good for me. I'm jet-lagged.

He drummed each of his fingers against the wheel.

OK. Just call me if it starts raining again, all right?

I got out of the car and he drove off without waving to me. My love for him felt so total and so annihilating that it was often impossible for me to see him clearly at all. If he left my line of sight for more than a few seconds, I couldn't even remember what his face looked like. I had read that infant animals formed attachments to inappropriate things sometimes, like falcons falling in love with their human breeders, or pandas with zookeepers, things like that. I once sent Nathan a list of articles about this phenomenon. Maybe I shouldn't have come to your christening, he replied.

Two years before, when I was twenty-two, we went to a family New Year's party together and came home very drunk in a taxi. I was still living with him then, finishing my undergraduate degree. Inside the door of his apartment, against the wall with the coat hooks, he kissed me. I felt feverish and stupid, like a thirsty person with too much water suddenly pouring into their mouth. Then he said in my ear: We really shouldn't do this. He was thirty-eight. That was it, he went to bed. We never kissed again. He even shrugged it off when I joked about it, the only time I could remember him being unkind to me. Did I do something? I said, after a few weeks. That made you want to stop, that time. My face was burning, I felt it. He winced. He didn't want to hurt me. He said no. It was over, that was it.

The hospital had a revolving door and smelled of disinfectant. Lights reflected garishly on the linoleum and people chatted and smiled, as if standing in the lobby of a theatre or university rather than a building for the sick and dying. Trying to be brave, I thought. And then I thought: or after a while it just becomes life again. I followed the signs upstairs and asked the nurses where Frank Doherty's room was. You must be his daughter, the blonde nurse said. Sukie, is it? My name is Amanda. You can follow me.

Outside Frank's room, Amanda helped me secure a plastic apron around my waist and tie a papery medical mask behind my ears. She explained that this was for Frank's benefit and not mine. His immune system was vulnerable and mine was not. I disinfected my hands with a cold, astringent alcohol rub and then Amanda opened the door. Your daughter is here, she said. A small man was sitting on the bed with bandaged feet. He had no hair and his skull was round like a pink pool ball. His mouth looked sore. Oh, I said. Well, hello!

At first I didn't know if he recognised me, though when I said my name he repeated it several times. I sat down. I asked if his brothers and sisters had been to see him; he couldn't seem to remember. He moved his thumbs back and forth compulsively, first one way, then another. This seemed to absorb so much attention that I wasn't sure he was even listening to me. Boston's nice, I said. Very cold this time of year. The Charles was frozen over when I left. I felt like I was presenting a radio show about travel to an uninterested audience. His thumbs moved back and forth, then forth and back. Frank? I said. He mumbled something, and I thought: well, even cats recognise their own names.

How are you feeling? I said.

He didn't answer the question. There was a small TV set fixed high up on the wall.

Do you watch much TV during the day? I said.

I thought he wasn't going to answer that, and then from nowhere he said: News.

You watch the news? I said. That went nowhere.

You're like your mother, Frank said.

I stared at him. I felt my body begin to go cold, or perhaps hot. Something happened to the temperature of my body that didn't feel good.

What do you mean?

Oh, you know what kind of person you are.

Do I?

You've got it all under control, said Frank. You're a cool customer. We'll see how cool you are when you're left on your own, hmm? Very cool you might be then.

Frank seemed to be addressing these remarks to the peripheral venous catheter taped to the skin of his left arm. He picked at it with a morbid aimlessness as he spoke. I heard my own voice grow wavery like a bad choral performance.

Why would I be left on my own? I said.

He'll go off and get married.

It was clear that Frank didn't know who I was. Realising this, I relaxed somewhat and wiped at my eyes over the edge of the paper mask. I was crying a little. We may as well have been two strangers talking about whether it would snow or not.

Maybe I'll marry him, I said.

At this Frank laughed, a performance without any apparent context, but which gratified me anyway. I loved to be rewarded with laughter.

Not a hope. He'll find some young one.

Younger than me?

Well, you're getting on, aren't you?

Then I laughed. Frank gave his IV line an avuncular smile.

But you're a decent girl, he said. Whatever they might say.

With this enigmatic truce our conversation ended. I tried to talk to him further, but he appeared too tired to engage, or too bored.

I stayed for an hour, though the visiting period lasted two. When I said I was leaving, Frank appeared not to notice. I left the room, closed the door carefully, and finally removed my paper mask and plastic apron. I held down the lever on the dispenser of disinfectant fluid until my hands were wet. It was cold, it stung. I rubbed them dry and then left the hospital. It was raining outside but I didn't call Nathan. I walked just like

I said I would, with my fur hat pulled down over my ears and my hands in my pockets.

As I approached Tara Street, I could see a little crowd had formed around the bridge and at the sides of the road. Their faces looked pink in the darkness and some of them were holding umbrellas, while above them Liberty Hall beamed down like a satellite. It was raining a weird, humid mist and a rescue boat was coming down the river with its lights on.

At first the crowd appeared vaguely wholesome, and I wondered if there was some kind of festive show happening, but then I saw what everybody was looking at: there was something floating in the river. I could see the slick cloth edge of it. It was the size of a human being. Nothing was wholesome or festive at all any more. The boat approached with its orange siren light revolving silently.

I didn't know whether to leave. I thought I probably didn't want to see a dead human body lifted out of the Liffey by a rescue boat. But I stayed put. I was standing next to a young Asian couple, a good-looking woman in an elegant black coat and a man who was speaking on the phone. They seemed to me like nice people, people who had been drawn into the drama of it all not for tawdry reasons but out of compassion. I felt better about being there when I noticed them.

The man on the rescue boat placed a pole with a hook down into the water, feeling for the edge of the object. Then he began to pull. We fell silent; even the man on the phone fell silent. Wordlessly the cloth pulled away, up with the hook, empty. For a moment there was confusion: was the body being stripped of its clothing? And then it became clear.

The cloth was the object. It was a sleeping bag floating on the surface of the river. The man went back to talking on the phone, and the woman in the coat started signalling something to him, something like: remember to ask what time. Everything was normal that quickly.

The rescue boat moved away and I stood with my elbows on the bridge, my blood-formation system working as usual, my cells maturing and dying at a normal rate. Nothing inside my body was trying to kill me. Death was, of course, the most ordinary thing that could happen, at some level I knew that. Still, I had stood there waiting to see the body in the river, ignoring the real living bodies all around me, as if death was more of a miracle than life was. I was a cold customer. It was too cold to think of things all the way through.

By the time I got back to the apartment the rain had soaked through my coat. In the hallway mirror my hat looked like a dirty water vole that might wake up at any second. I removed it along with my coat. Sukie? Nathan said from inside. I smoothed down my hair into an acceptable shape. How did it go? he said. I walked inside. He was sitting on the couch, holding the TV remote in his right hand. You're drowned, he said. Why didn't you call me?

I said nothing.

Was it bad? Nathan said.

I nodded. My face was cold, burning with cold, red like a traffic light. I went into my room and peeled off my wet clothes to hang them up. They were heavy, and held the shape of my body in their creases. I brushed my hair flat and put on my embroidered dressing gown so that I felt clean and composed. This is what human beings do with their lives, I thought. I took one hard disciplinary breath and then went back out to the living room.

Nathan was watching TV, but he hit the mute button when I came out. I got onto the couch beside him and closed my eyes while he reached over to touch my hair. We used to watch films together like that, and he would touch my hair in that exact way, distractedly. I found his distraction comforting. In a way I wanted to live inside it, as if it was a place of its own, where he would never notice I had entered. I thought of saying: I don't want to go back to Boston. I want to live here with you. But instead I said: Put the sound back on if you're watching it, I don't mind.

He hit the button again and the sound

came back, tense string music and a female voice gasping. A murder, I thought. But when I opened my eyes it was a sex scene. She was on her hands and knees and the male character was behind her.

I like it like that, I said. From behind, I mean. That way I can pretend it's you.

Nathan coughed, he lifted his hand away from my hair. But after a second he said: Generally I just close my eyes. The sex scene was over now. They were in a courtroom instead. I felt my mouth watering.

Can we fuck? I said. But seriously.

Yeah, I knew you were going to say that.

It would make me feel a lot better.

Jesus Christ, said Nathan.

Then we lapsed into silence. The conversation waited for our return. I had calmed down, I could see that. Nathan touched my ankle and I developed a casual interest in the plot of the television drama.

It's not a good idea, Nathan said.

Why not? You're in love with me, aren't you?

Infamously.

It's one small favour, I said.

No. Paying for your flight home was a small favour. We're not going to argue about this. It's not a good idea.

In bed that night I asked him: When will we know if this was a bad idea or not? Should we already know? Because now it feels good.

No, now is too early, he said. I think when you get back to Boston we'll have more perspective.

I'm not going back to Boston, I didn't say. *These cells may look fairly normal, but they are not.*